I Can Read! Phonics

SPIDER SENSE®
SPIDER-MAN

PHONICS FUN!

Features short and long vowel sounds

I Can Read! Phonics

SPIDER SENSE SPIDER-MAN

PHONICS FUN!

Features short and long vowel sounds

TABLE OF CONTENTS

Letter to Parents

Dear Parents,

Your child is about to start an exciting adventure. He or she is going to learn to read. By choosing your child's favorite characters, you have already accomplished something very important—motivation!

Spider-Man Phonics Fun includes twelve storybooks, planned by a phonics expert. The books are intended for children to read at home with a parent or caregiver and, eventually, by themselves.

- *Spider-Man Phonics Fun* introduces long and short vowel sounds. One of the key components in becoming a fluent reader is practice, so this set features one book for each sound, plus one introductory story, and one book that reinforces all the sounds. Learning to read long and short vowels is rewarding because they are found everywhere!
- Fun Spider-Man words have been included to make the stories rich and enjoyable.
- The stories also include sight words. These are words frequently found in books that can be hard to sound out. They just need to be learned by sight!
- Picture clues support the text in each story and help children learn new words.

As children master the sounds and words, they will gain experience and confidence in their ability to understand sounds, sound out words, and READ! Here are some suggestions for using *Spider-Man Phonics Fun* to help your child on the road to reading:

1. Read the books aloud to your child. The first time you read a story, read it all the way through. Then invite your child to follow along by pointing out words as you read them. Encourage him or her to try to sound out new words that use familiar sounds, or that are pictured in the illustrations.

2. Discuss each sound found on the first page with your child. Help your child sound out the new words in the story. Demonstrate the vowel sounds—for example, by telling your child that the short **o** vowel sound is found in the word **hot**.

3. Look at the pictures with your child. Encourage him or her to tell the story through the pictures. Point out objects in the pictures and ask your child to name them.

We hope that you and your child enjoy *Spider-Man Phonics Fun*, and that it is the start of many happy reading adventures.

The HarperCollins Editors

SPIDER SENSE
SPIDER-MAN®

MEET THE VILLAINS
Book 1 • Introduction

Written by Lucy Rosen
Phonics scope and sequence by Cathy Toohey
Pictures by Andie Tong & Jeremy Roberts and MADA Design, Inc.

In this story you will learn new sight words.
Can you find these words?

all	has	off
always	into	one
and	is	the
are	laugh	to
around	lots	too
big	many	when
but	not	
comes	of	

Spider-Man knows

lots of bad guys.

They always make trouble.

The Green Goblin likes
to laugh, but his jokes
are not funny.

The Rhino puts up
one big fight when he
comes into town.

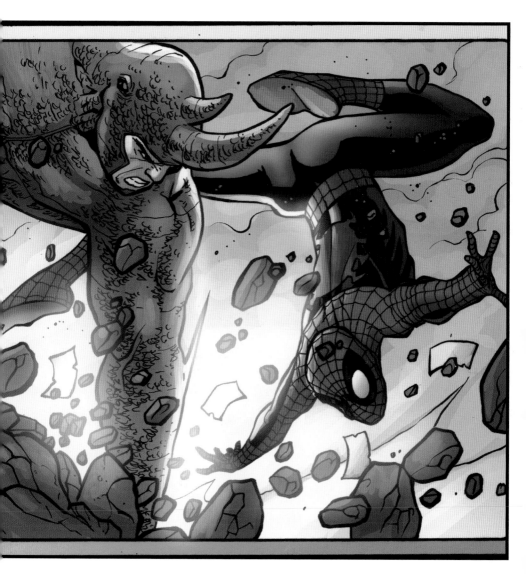

The Vulture is always
flying around the city.

Doc Ock has too many arms and no manners.

Can Spider-Man fight off all of these foes?

SPIDER SENSE
SPIDER-MAN

SPIDER-MAN VERSUS THE LIZARD
Book 2 • Short a

Written by Lucy Rosen
Phonics scope and sequence by Cathy Toohey
Pictures by MADA Design, Inc.

In this story you will learn about the **short a** vowel sound. Can you find these words and sound them out?

am	crashed	plan
back	fast	thrash
can	handy	zagged
catch	lab	
crash	man	

Here are some sight words:

a	if	said	too
he	into	to	

Here are some fun Spider-Man words:

creature   potion   strange

Peter heard a loud crash.

"What was that?" he said.

"I am the Lizard,"

said a strange creature.

"I used to be a man.

Now catch me if you can!"

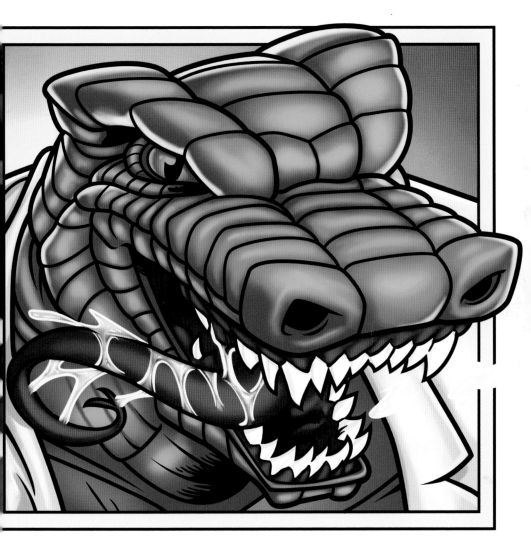

Spider-Man tried to catch the Lizard. He zigged and he zagged. But the Lizard was too fast.

"I need a new plan,"
said Spidey.
He found a lab nearby.
"That's handy," he said.

The Lizard crashed into the lab. He drank from Spidey's glass. The Lizard began to thrash.

The potion worked! The Lizard was a man again. "Glad to have you back," said Spidey.

SPIDER SENSE
SPIDER-MAN®

THE
MENACE OF THE MOLTEN MAN
Book 3 • Short e

Written by Lucy Rosen
Phonics scope and sequence by Cathy Toohey
Pictures by Andie Tong & Jeremy Roberts

In this story you will learn about the **short e** vowel sound. Can you find these words and sound them out?

clever	melted	vent
end	mess	web
enemy	metal	webbing
head	pest	
jet	red	

Here are some sight words:

| a | from | once | the | until |
| caught | he | some | to | was |

Here are some fun Spider-Man words:

meteorite   scientist   strange

Mark was once a clever scientist, until he touched some strange metal.

Mark became the Molten Man! He was Spider-Man's enemy.

Molten Man wanted to steal
a meteorite. But Spider-Man
knew he had to stop him.
"I caught you red-handed!"
said Spidey.

Spidey shot a web at Molten Man, but the web melted away. "What a mess," said Spider-Man.

A jet of cold air
blasted from a vent.
It chilled Molten Man
from head to toe.

Spider-Man's webbing worked now. "There's the end of that pest!" said Spider-Man.

SPIDER SENSE
SPIDER-MAN®

SPIDER-MAN VERSUS THE VULTURE
Book 4 • Short i

Written by Lucy Rosen
Phonics scope and sequence by Cathy Toohey
Pictures by Andie Tong & Jeremy Roberts

In this story you will learn about the **short i** vowel sound. Can you find these words and sound them out?

city	**hit**	**thing**
dipped	**quick**	**think**
grin	**silver**	**trick**
him	**spin**	**wings**

Here are some sight words:

over   **the**   **you**

Here is a fun Spider-Man word:

invention

Spider-Man saw the

Vulture fly over the city.

"I'm stealing this silver," said the Vulture with a grin. "Try to stop me!"

Spider-Man tried to hit the Vulture with a web. The Vulture dipped out of the way.

"Those wings make him too quick for me," said Spider-Man. "But I know just the thing to stop him."

"Let's take my invention out for a spin," said Spidey. A beam split the Vulture's wings.

"Hey, Vulture!" said Spider-Man.
"Nice trick, don't you think?"

SPIDER SENSE
SPIDER-MAN®

SPIDER-MAN VERSUS ELECTRO
Book 5 • Short o

Written by Lucy Rosen
Phonics scope and sequence by Cathy Toohey
Pictures by MADA Design, Inc.

In this story you will learn about the **short o** vowel sound. Can you find these words and sound them out?

cops	**job**	**shocked**
costume	**not**	**solve**
drop	**popped**	**spot**
gosh	**problem**	**stop**
got	**rob**	

Here are some sight words:

a	**his**	**of**	**was**
him	**into**	**the**	**when**

Here is a fun Spider-Man word:

scary

Peter was walking to his job when something made him stop.

"I am Electro," said a scary man.

"I will rob the city of its power!"

"Gosh," said Peter.

"That's not nice!"

Peter got into his
Spider-Man costume.
He found Electro's
hiding spot.

"Shocked to see me, Electro?"
Spidey said.

Electro hissed and popped.

"You can't stop me!" he yelled.

"A drop of water

can solve this problem,"

said Spider-Man.

"Looks like you've got a date

with the cops!" Spider-Man said.

SPIDER SENSE
SPIDER-MAN®

SPIDER-MAN VERSUS KRAVEN
Book 6 • Short u

Written by Lucy Rosen
Phonics scope and sequence by Cathy Toohey
Pictures by Andie Tong & Jeremy Roberts

In this story you will learn about the **short u** vowel sound. Can you find these words and sound them out?

ducked	**hunter**	**punched**
fun	**jumped**	**spun**
hungry	**jungle**	**sunset**
hunt	**luck**	**until**
hunted	**much**	

Here are some sight words:

a   for   his   the   to   was

Here are some fun Spider-Man words:

attack   finally

Kraven the Hunter
was hungry for a fight.
But he waited until sunset
to start his attack.

"I live by the law
of the jungle," said Kraven.
"Hunt or be hunted."

"That doesn't sound like much fun," said Spider-Man.

Spider-Man punched hard.

Kraven ducked.

Spider-Man jumped

on Kraven's back.

Finally Spidey spun his webs all around Kraven. "You're out of luck!" he said.

SPIDER SENSE
SPIDER-MAN®

THE GREAT HOLIDAY CHASE
Book 7 • Long a

Written by Lucy Rosen
Phonics scope and sequence by Cathy Toohey
Pictures by MADA Design, Inc.

In this story you will learn about the **long a** vowel sound. Can you find these words and sound them out?

aim	display	safe
away	late	saved
case	paying	take
chased	place	
day	raced	

Here are some sight words:

on   the   then   through   to   was

Here are some fun Spider-Man words:

diamond   holiday   whisked

Silver Sable was trying to take the city's Holiday Diamond. But Spider-Man was on the case.

Silver Sable raced through the mall. "That diamond must be somewhere in this place," she said.

Spider-Man chased Silver
Sable. Then she saw the
diamond on display.
"You're too late!"
said Silver Sable.

"Hey, Silver Sable,"
said Spider-Man.
"You can't just take a
diamond without paying!"

Spider-Man took careful aim.

He shot a web and whisked

the diamond away.

The diamond was safe.

Spidey saved the day!

SPIDER SENSE
SPIDER-MAN®

MEET SPIDER-MAN
Book 8 • Long e

Written by Lucy Rosen
Phonics scope and sequence by Cathy Toohey
Pictures by Andie Tong & Jeremy Roberts

In this story you will learn about the **long e** vowel sound. Can you find these words and sound them out?

beat	free	people
became	he	Peter
being	hero	secret
believe	keep	speed
easy	meet	
evil	needs	

Here are some sight words:

a   has   his   is   was

Here are some fun Spider-Man words:

powers   regular

Meet Spider-Man.

Spider-Man has a secret.

His real name

is Peter Parker.

Before he became a hero,
Peter was just a regular kid.
Now Peter is a teenager
with powers.

Spider-Man uses his strength and speed to keep the city free of crime.

Being a hero isn't easy.
There are a lot of
evil guys to beat.

But people believe in Spider-Man.

The city needs its Super Hero!

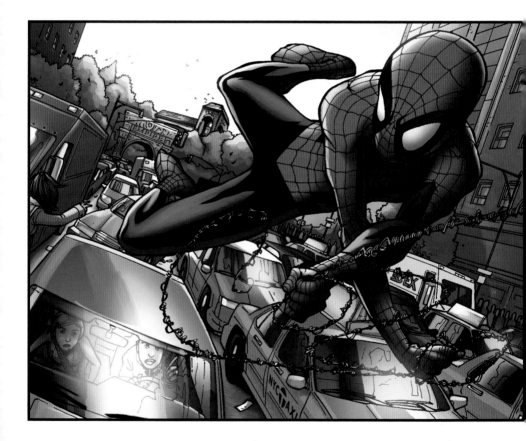

SPIDER SENSE
SPIDER-MAN®

CLASH WITH THE RHINO
Book 9 • Long i

Written by Lucy Rosen
Phonics scope and sequence by Cathy Toohey
Pictures by Andie Tong & Jeremy Roberts

In this story you will learn about the **long i** vowel sound. Can you find these words and sound them out?

behind	hiding	right
cried	inside	spider
crime	life	tied
fight	might	time
find	night	tried
hi	rhino	untied

Here are some sight words:

a   had   he   him   is   this

Here are some fun Spider-Man words:

committed   **kidnapped**

The Rhino committed
an awful crime.
He kidnapped the
mayor's son.

"I must find out where the Rhino is hiding," said Spider-Man. "My spider-sense tells me this might be the right place."

Spidey crashed inside.

The Rhino was behind him.

"Hi there, evil guy," said

Spider-Man. "Your time is up."

"Not on your life!"

cried the Rhino.

The Rhino tried to fight,
but Spider-Man
tied him up.

Spidey untied the boy.

"What a night!" he said.

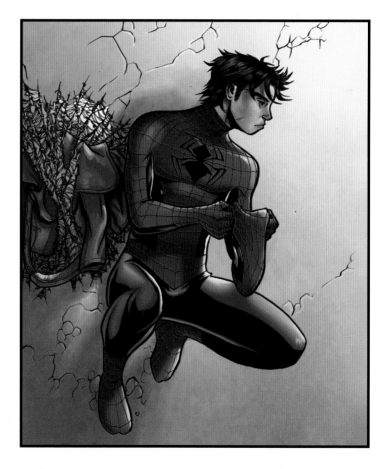

SPIDER SENSE
SPIDER-MAN®

SPIDER-MAN VERSUS THE GREEN GOBLIN

Book 10 • Long o

Written by Lucy Rosen
Phonics scope and sequence by Cathy Toohey
Pictures by Andie Tong & Jeremy Roberts

In this story you will learn about the **long o** vowel sound. Can you find these words and sound them out?

clothes	low	rolled
cold	old	show
foe	over	smoke
go	police	throw
going	road	

Here are some sight words:

a   he   it   was

Here are some fun Spider-Man words:

bombs   knocked   police

Spider-Man swung over the city. "Where are you going?" asked a man in funny clothes.

It was Spidey's old foe,

the Green Goblin.

"Let's get this show on the road," said the Goblin. He started to throw smoke bombs at Spider-Man.

But Spidey rolled out of the smoke. "Where did the Goblin go?" said Spider-Man.

"Over here!" said the Goblin.
Spider-Man swung down
low and knocked the Goblin
out cold.

"Show's over," said Spider-Man.

"Time to go to the police!"

SPIDER SENSE
SPIDER-MAN®

BATTLE WITH DOC OCK
Book 11 • -sh and -ch blends

Written by Lucy Rosen
Phonics scope and sequence by Cathy Toohey
Pictures by Andie Tong & Jeremy Roberts

In this story you will learn about the **-ch** and **-sh** sounds. Can you find these words and sound them out?

catch	**reach**	**teach**
chased	**research**	**touch**
crush	**shot**	**trash**

Here are some sight words:

a	**from**	**his**
and	**he**	**was**

Here is a fun Spider-Man word:

powers

Doc Ock was a
hard guy to catch.

With his metal arms,

Doc Ock could reach, touch,

and crush almost anything.

One day, Spider-Man
saw Doc Ock
using his powers to steal
some research from a lab.

"Time to teach you a lesson," said Spidey.

Spider-Man chased Doc Ock.

He shot his webs.

Soon, Doc Ock was tied up.

"Time to call the cops,"
said Spidey.

"Looks like someone took out the trash," said the police.

SPIDER SENSE
SPIDER-MAN®

A DAY IN THE LIFE OF
PETER PARKER
Book 12 • Review

Written by Lucy Rosen
Phonics scope and sequence by Cathy Toohey
Pictures by Andie Tong & Jeremy Roberts

In this story you will review the short vowel sounds. Can you find these words and sound them out?

after	get	not
bad	has	pest
boss	his	snaps
but	in	upset
can	job	with
city	lives	yell
enemy	lot	

Here are some sight words:

a   be   he   is   to

Here are some fun Spider-Man words:

aunt   newspaper   school

Peter lives in
New York City
with his aunt May.

Peter has a job
after school.

Peter snaps photos
for the newspaper.

Peter's boss can be mean.

He likes to yell a lot.

But Peter does not get upset.

Mr. Jameson can be a pest, but he is not Peter's enemy.

Peter knows a lot of bad guys.

That is because Peter is Spider-Man

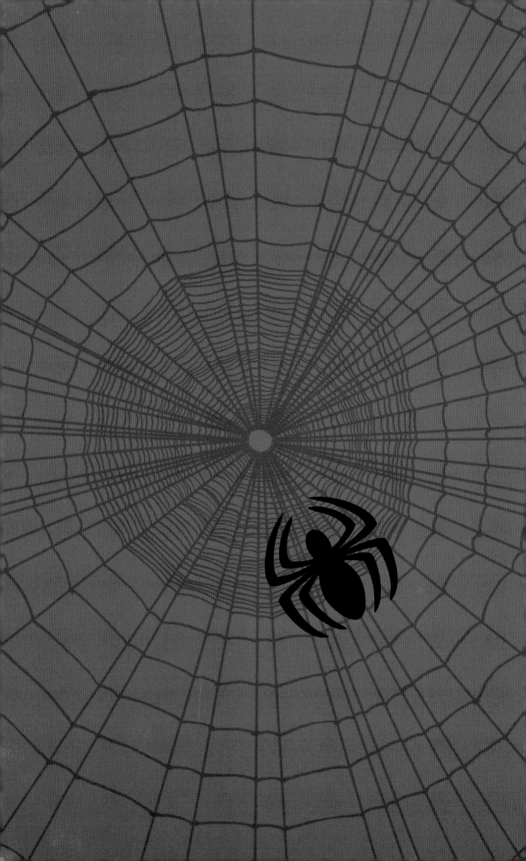